... the one, who just recently sincerely believed that he was in charge of something, suddenly appears to be lying prone and motionless in a wooden box, and his associates, realizing that the deceased is of no use for them anymore, burn him in the furnace.

"The Master and Margarita", M. Bulgakov.

Introduction

Praise the Lord, the Creator of all things, and the Creator of all the worlds.

I dedicate this book to my daughter Raphael.

I wrote this book as a humble endeavor to change the mentality of humankind in the whole world. I want my children to live a spiritual life with faith in God as a permanent priority in their minds, and the material aspect should never affect the decisions of my children.

Lucifer

Worlds are ruled by the power or energy that the people of the planet Earth name the Lord God.

Accordingly, God is the Light, and Satan is the darkness. So most people believe. But what do we know about Satan? Where did Satan come from, and what is his relationship with God? If you believe the Holy Writings, then Satan, Iblis, the Devil was created by God to be His right hand, and he was the first Archangel among other archangels. The Romans called him Lucifer – the one who carries the Light. Nevertheless, according to priests' propagation, the Devil stinks of tar and sulfur, his dreadful horns and hooves grow from goat head and wooly legs, so how possibly can he carry the Light?

It does not come together to form a whole somehow. I think that the truth looks different; this truth will upset the Church authorities, who admire expensive things and love exquisite clothes. The truth is that Lucifer now and always serves God only. If God had created Lucifer, then how could Lucifer contradict his Creator? However, Lucifer never doubted God; only human souls doubted Him. The priests, who have sworn to serve God, buy exclusive cars for themselves, live in luxurious houses, wear jewelry made of solid gold, and at the same time they dissemble and dodge, and sin in the sight of the Lord. The Devil has nothing to do with it.

Lucifer offered and still offers people various options and suggestions, and they, realizing that they often choose the wrong way, blame Lucifer for everything, who, by the Will of the Most High, discharges his duties very thoroughly and obediently.

What will we feel after death? It will be pain. It will be the pain of recognizing that we did not live righteously and spent our given time in vain, and missed our chance to get closer to God. Our souls will judge us by our deeds. Moreover, most likely they will themselves pray God to return them to the Earth once again and pass the trials anew, to correct the former mistakes and redeem their sins. That would last forever until we learn the lesson, so we should always do the right thing in the proper time. For those who had read Mikhail Bulgakov's *The Master and Margarita,* it is evident, that this state is similar to the woeful fate of Pilate, who desired to return the time back and waited thousands of years to implore forgiveness for his cowardice. And the words that did not leave him all that time were the words of Yeshua Ha-Notsri – Jesus of Nazareth – ***'Cowardice is certainly one of the most terrible vices'***…

He begged God to turn back time. This was a strong pain. One can betray only once.

The Qur'an teaches that we should ***'Never speak aloud'***. This refers to your plans, to speaking about other people, because Iblis is standing next to you, he will immediately check on you. You should not say anything aloud, neither good nor bad. If it is bad, then Iblis will surely check on you and send you a trial that you would not expect, and if it is good, he will take it away from you very easily. The territory of the Earth is the hell itself; it is a prison for our souls. God teaches us not to speak aloud and not to give Iblis additional work.

I can say about myself that I can both love and hate. I can save a person; I can cripple him. I can be an angel; I can be a demon.

So how to decide? I am a simple mortal man, for someone, I am an angel, and for someone else, I am an infinite evil and a demon. Who switches this mode? Who controls us and other forces? Is it not the Lord God Himself? Therefore, it is very important to live a spiritual life in order not to commit misconduct, for which we will have to answer with the sufferings of our soul. Prayer to God is the water with which we wash our soul from filth. We wash our body so as not to smell, meanwhile forgetting about our soul. When we open our soul to God, tears appear in our eyes, this means that we are on the right path.

My dear friends, my most favorite biblical story is the telling about Job, who was devotedly faithful to God. The story of Job is the story about how Satan implicitly serves the Lord God and fulfills the Will of the Lord. No ministers of the church like this story because it contradicts their propagation about the nasty devil with dreadful horns and hooves. Many people do not want to change their habitual belief and live in mispersuasion, but the Devil is not a stubborn goat, the Devil is present everywhere. The Devil is money or a beautiful girl who seduces, the Devil is a bank that gives almost gift loans, and the Devil is a casino where they offer you a fabulous life. Lucifer is the greatest master of delusion.

"The devil's greatest trick is to convince you that he does not exist."

Charles Baudelaire

The so-called exorcism is a very blatant deception. That means that there are some invisible forces obsessing a human person, a creature of a lower order and manifest their will, imposing it on the poor devil. Then comes another man who with simple words expels the Devil or a demon. This nonsense is intended for children or people who are not intelligent enough. We, common people, who cannot properly control ourselves, can manage higher powers with words. This is very naive. We are fragile and vulnerable and only God can help us, but no one else. We must realize this fact in time to avoid troubles.

The Devil, Satan, Iblis, Lucifer carrying the Light, are different names of the so-called impure evil force. Why impure? This is because people have scant imagination. How can a creature of fire be impure? The fire is pure and clean. All angels and archangels are made of the matter of fire, or most likely, of the matter, about which we know nothing. The matter that may be invisible to our eyes, and can take any shape.

Lucifer is the Archangel of the Lord God, he does not stink of sulfur, and he certainly does not harm people without the permission of the Lord God. Lucifer is not evil himself; he simply provides a person with the opportunity to choose with the permission of God.

In any case, either angels or demons do absolutely nothing without God's permission to do something one way or another. I even see it differently, there are no demons and no devils, and there are only angels who fulfill the will of the Lord. If an angel kills a man, we say that a demon or a devil did it. But if this same force saves a man, then we say that it is an angel. That is simply power or energy, which fulfills the Will of God.

Although there is a possibility that the world in which we find ourselves is just an illusion, and our souls 'dream' about our life on the Earth. A real dream about a virtual reality. After such a dream, our behavior is being analyzed. The truth we do not know, the truth is hidden from us. However, I am sure that 'the evil Devil' does not exist, only 'Lucifer' is possible, who performs only what the Lord God commands. Lucifer was able to take everything from Job, but then Lucifer multiplied what was taken away from Job and gave him even more than he took. If we could understand the principle of the work of God and His Creations, then people would make fewer mistakes. Moreover, this 'hell on the Earth' would become much better. I want people to understand that there is no evil; Lucifer is the Archangel, same as Michael or Gabriel. And just like Gabriel kills according to the will of God, so does any other Angel or Archangel.

The question of money. In the world with God, money does not exist, in our human world, we have plenty of everything, and we want to achieve abundance in this life by any means. This is where we are caught all the time.

Money is the invention of the Devil, and with this tool, the Devil tests and probes us, according to the Will of the Lord. The test by money is the most problematic trial that God gives us with the help of his servant Lucifer. People perform the most terrible crimes because of money, cheat, steal, rob and kill. Only when we completely ignore wealth and accept our destiny the way God gives it to us, only then there is the opportunity of rehabilitation, the possibility occurs that God will forgive us our sins and will not bring us back to the Earth after we die. We make many mistakes because of our ambitions and emotions, and because of money, and mistakes return us back to our life on the Earth in a new body.

The idea of this book is to help each person get priorities straight. The problem is that we only believe in what we see with our own eyes, so most people do not believe in God and in eternal life outside the Earth.

The Earth is the territory of Lucifer. The planet Earth is an interstellar ship, Lucifer is the captain of the ship, and God is the Great Creator of all things, the Creator of both ships and captains. Satan rules the mundane world on the Earth, and the Lord God allows this, this is a test for our souls. The souls are tested in hell, and being on Earth is hell. Our souls are shackled in our bodies. On the Earth, we are surrounded by deception everywhere. The Earth is a planet of delusions. The Devil's staff is everywhere, they surround us test our communication with God. The material world is the world of Satan. The Devil checks everyone.

And if everyone could understand this, there would be no war, no hunger, no killing. This is the plan of the Lord God, and it is not for me, a simple servant of God to change the charter. With all my soul, I want to make our world one, so that our Universe is one. God gives to each according to his needs; each soul receives what is necessary for it in order to strengthen its connection with God. Since our thoughts are material, I have not lost everything yet, and still have chances.

Therefore, I will commence my reflections from the Bible and our misconceptions about our world and about God. In most cases, people like to discuss others, on this principle the whole society is built, where the courts and various correctional organizations constantly work. However, if each of us would know that by punishing a stranger, we punish ourselves and hurt ourselves too, I am sure that prisons would cease to exist. The Bible very clearly and accessibly says,

This is the golden rule of morality. Moreover, this golden rule must be understood and taken literally.

Note that the faithful servant of the Lord God Lucifer has absolutely nothing to do with our troubles. Firstly, mainly, and exclusively, the Lord God is the only power that decides absolutely everything, the fate, and deeds of everyone, including angels and mortal people and Lucifer himself. Lucifer will never act without the approval of the Lord God; this is also clearly written in the Bible. The best example is the story of good Job, mentioned above. Job was a righteous God-fearing man, wholeheartedly devoted to the Lord. The angels told God so and rejoiced for Job, but Satan, who was standing next to the angels, began to doubt Job's decency and loyalty. Satan saw that Job lived very well and happily, and therefore he doubted Job's decency. Moreover, he suggested God take away from him his wealth for the beginning, then family and friends, and eventually, health, in a word, everything but life. Therefore, God gave permission for Satan's actions; God entrusted Job's destiny to Satan. God allowed Satan to take everything away from Job and check on Job's behavior, would Job remain as God-fearing and faithful as ever, or would he blaspheme.

Eventually, it all ended well for Job. Job has stoically endured all the trials. Then God ordered Satan, 'Give Job everything back in multiple!' Satan obediently fulfilled the Will of the Lord. Why no one cites this case as an example, in proof that the Devil, Satan, Lucifer is not the enemy of the Lord God, but is simply the prosecutor of humankind. Lucifer, which is translated from Latin as 'carrying the Light', who is also called Satan is the faithful servant of the Lord God.

Nevertheless, I am sure that is all conventional... God does not speak to anyone; God knows everything. He controls everything around without words. Man, created by the Lord from clay, is a weak creature, weak-willed and weak-minded. Satan is able to embellish bad things, and people are tempted by empty colorful candy wrappers like the aborigines on the newly discovered lands. God punished our souls and imprisoned them in our bodies, and, dwelling in punishment, we create still more misfortunes for ourselves, thereby prolonging our horrible life on the Earth. The concept of reincarnation has long been known and it explains to us why terrible things happen to young and innocent children; the body is young, but the soul is old and sinful, which deserves pain and punishment. We are in hell. The Earth is hell. Words from The Qur'an, like the words in any holy letter, must be taken literally,

Thus, we, people, create this hell for ourselves with our own hands, stealing, deceiving and killing each other, in a vain hope to improve our life. Consequently, wrong behavior prolongs our stay on this Earth. That means the eternal hell; every wrong deed alienates us from God and from real freedom, that freedom that we do not remember.

In order to gain that real freedom, the man should live his life with dignity, so that God would eventually establish him near Himself.

In the great Bulgakov's masterpiece *The Master and Margarita*, Satan appears in the image of Woland. Through the whole novel duplicitous Woland mocks at envious average citizens, at human oscitancy, and at limited common mentality. In addition, not only Bulgakov created this character. There are many different images of one mighty force, who is Satan. Let us follow what the evil cunning Devil Woland says. The primary thing is that God exists; Jesus Christ also exists. Woland says that people themselves do not decide anything in this life and cannot even manage their lives.

1. Yes, a man is mortal, but that would be half the trouble. The worst thing is that he is sometimes suddenly mortal, that is the trick! And in general, he cannot even say what he will do tonight.

2. For no reason at all, no brick will ever fall on someone's head.

3. How can a person be in charge of anything, if he is not only deprived of the opportunity to project some simple plan for at least a ridiculously short period, well, let's say, a thousand years, but cannot even vouch for his own tomorrow?

4. ... the one, who just recently sincerely believed that he was in charge of something, suddenly appears to be lying prone and motionless in a wooden box, and his associates, realizing that the deceased is of no use for them anymore, burn him in the furnace.

5. ... but here is the question that bothers me: if there is no God, then, I wonder, who controls human life and everything in general on earth?

No matter how strange it may seem, we don't even take pains to think about it. We believe that we will live forever; especially, rich people who want to be immortal, think so. I can give lots of examples.

God creates murderers, born killers who have always killed, both in the past life and in this one. This is their doom. Therefore, it is strange that such killers live without problems in a society with their families; no one perceives them as a danger. Everyone thinks that he speaks with a common person, but he already speaks with his own death. Every murderer lives as his heart says, and God says to every murderer, 'don't touch him.' Or 'kill him today', or 'ax this bastard in a month.' This is how God sets up his network, invisible network. It happens right away. Should a person say aloud that there is no God, or that he is God himself, as packs of crocodiles, sharks, birds of prey and ravaging maniacs immediately rush to him, raven   after someone to kill, though they still do not know whom, and suddenly see him – this 'earthen god'. The killer never simply kills anyone. A pigeon never simply crap on one. And all holy scriptures say about it, for example, the Vedic *Bhagavad Gita* in a dialogue between Pandava prince Arjuna and The Almighty Krishna in disguise of his guide and charioteer, as well as in a story about the biblical Moses whose bunch has killed bundles of other ancient Jews who had crafted the golden bull... Why does God kill people? God is preparing for every earthly person a new destiny, and this new destiny may be even worse than the previous one. Thus, a tycoon who does not deserve his well-off life because of his wrongdoings dies and is reborn as a little dark-skinned child in a deserted corner somewhere in Africa, where there is no food, and no water. Where this little black kid will suffer very much, the little black kid will be permanently hungry and constantly ill. This little black kid will suffer greatly and die of hunger. So why did this happen? Because, in a past life, this small, poor and sick black kid was a brazen white rich rascal who threw away tons of food in the trash and hardened in sin and blasphemy. Everything is interconnected, so no one should be sorry. Everyone has earned his own destiny. To avoid falling into the trap, one should think twice and consider well his words and deeds. Angels stand nearby, listen, and look after each person.

And our foe, Lucifer-Satan, is in an await of our mistakes. Everything is well written in the Qur'an. The saying goes as ***'Never speak aloud'.*** That is, if we think, then our thoughts remain between God and us; and when we speak loudly, then our words can hear everyone, including Satan. And after the words, an additional trial follows.

The great poet and philosopher Goethe wrote his masterpiece Faust. In this novel, we recognize Satan in the appearance of Mephistopheles. Mephistopheles as Woland also probes Faust, a great scientist. Mephistopheles mocks everyone too, in this case, Professor Faust, who, being a man of an outstanding analytical mind nevertheless falls into the foe's trap. It is incommensurate to compare earthly, worldly pondering with Satan's divine, eternal, and true thinking. God illuminates the minds of not everyone because one must deserve wisdom by the desire to get close to God. How many of you sincerely praised God for water, food, shelter over your head, who of you knelt in church or just outside and prayed to God? Nobody turns to God, everyone eats, drinks, mates and everyone thinks that this is how it should be. Then when a sudden illness comes, only Satan is to blame for this and you need a talisman or a fortuneteller to avert the evil eye. Generally speaking, isn't it absurd that some hoodoo fortuneteller drives Satan away? How to explain to commons that Satan is not interested in straight decent people?

Proper nutrition and a lively lifestyle lead to the condition when our body does not create problems for us, or creates fewer problems, so we can devote more time to spiritual matters. The saying *'healthy mind in a healthy body'* is very relevant and corresponds to reality. A fat decent person is rare to meet. Fat people are busy with their rectum; there main interest lies in how and with what to fill their stomachs. This observation definitely and categorically applies to alcoholics and drug addicts; all these people are estranged from God and think only about themselves.

Our body should be a strong and clean vessel for our soul. When the current conductivity in our body is high, then it is easy for the soul to get in touch with God. Then we are not susceptible and whimsical both to nutrition and to external factors, we become stress-resistant in any situation. Communication with God is highly intensive, and we begin to see the real world, we feel people, we distinguish lies. Intuition becomes perfect.

Smoking is also very harmful. We must remain clean and regularly thank God for all that He has given us. With prayer, we wash away the filth from our souls. Therefore, it is necessary to pray every day, as well as wash your hands. In Islam, this is Wudu, washing with water before namaz; we wash both the body and our soul. A dirty soul attracts troubles to itself; they fly like flies to dung. What does trouble mean? Trouble means a trial that we cannot avoid.

In reality, there are occurrences that happen seemingly without a motive. Notorious Breivik killed 77 people and injured 151 during his violent attack. This is another example of a person who had dissociated himself from God and did not understand all the responsibility that fell on him. Although, God allowed these people to fall victims to Breivik. Simultaneously God sends probation to everyone. If Breivik had not shot these people, they would have died anyway. It is fate. It was their doom. If God would not wish them to die, Breivik would not be born. Or he would have died in an accident. The Will of the Lord God is above all.

Death itself is not something bad, death is a pleasant journey for mature souls, and for the immature ones it is transportation to hard labor. It depends on what stage of development this soul is. Regarding the murder, in this case, the situation can be compared to that described in *Bhagavad Gita*, in Krishna's dialogue with Arjuna. Arjuna evaded the fight against his brothers, so Krishna revealed himself as the Almighty and told Arjuna that the life of his brothers had already been decided, and even if Arjuna would not kill them, they were still doomed to be dead. Their bodies were soaked, and they would die anyway, even if Arjuna would not raise his sword on them. Anyway, everything has been decided already without Arjuna's participation. This is a test and education for every soul. In any case, everyone will return to God, eventually, it does not depend on us.

Now the time has come, for each of us. We returned to God. Our souls did not want to leave the abode of God, but we needed to go through hell without memory to show the power of attraction to God. This is a blind attraction; it resembles the force of a magnet. God removed our memories, but we still remembered Him and returned to Him. Moreover, all these religious teachings are utter nonsense for trying to confuse and distance us from God. The Church or the Mosque is a tool of Lucifer to intimidate ordinary people; God Allah created these institutions with the help of the cunning Iblis the Devil. These religious structures repel us from God and turn the teachings of the Lord into a venom. The church is stuffy and smells of incense and stinks of sweaty half-insane men in cassocks; and the mosque emanates an open outward hostility. The parsons and imams are definitely and clearly the servants of the Devil. In these temples, a church or a mosque alike, gather mostly deceitful people busy gossiping and picking other people to pieces. In such places, there is no God. These people are deceiving themselves and deceiving others, they as true servants of the Devil, confuse common people and send them on a false slippery path. As for Christianity, here Lucifer did his best to devote much effort to the creation of outrageous postulates of Catholicism and Orthodoxy.

Oh, Catholics, bastards of Satan, homosexuals and pedophiles, traitors and police agents! You all are in first ranks of dishonor near the Devil!

So, here is a step by step instruction. The priest in the Catholic Church has no right to marry; as a result, celibate turns him into a blatant homosexual and pedophile. The Catholic Church waged hundreds of bloody wars and killed in most cruel terrific ways many innocent people who contradicted their satanic teaching.

Yes, I affirm that the gospel is the teaching of Lucifer in order to confuse and enslave the people. Why do they not like Islam? Do not like Muslims? Because it is the Religion from God, which severely punishes for sins and does not ask a person to endure injustice. People are predatory creatures, whom the Institute of the Church is trying to enslave and turn sin into an insignificant matter. We are not herbivores, we are predators, and if mortal punishment were allowed in our society, there would be less crime. What does the church teach us? If they hit you on the left cheek, turn the right one, give all you have away and stay in the wind like a naked fool. What does the Qur'an teach? If they hit you with the left hand, hit back with your right hand. When everyone knows these rules, no one wants to beat another. What causes confusion? Disorder breeds mayhem. Everyone knows that to steal or deceive another person, will pass unpunished if you have money. There are mostly herbivores, chained people around us; they will be reborn many times until they dare to throw off the shackles. Someday they will just get tired of injustice. What is freedom? I will tell you from my own example.

It happened in 1999. In some stupid way, I have made me some acquaintances among German criminals in hope to earn a couple of German marks. I tried, but my work was not paid. But one case changed me completely, at the DNA level, I recognized who I was.

<u>**I am a predator.**</u> And this is what one should not be afraid of, or be shy, people just will not deceive you anymore, ever. The state loves herbivorous slaves who are easy to deceive and rape. They are afraid to harm you because they know that you will severely punish them.

Thus, some scoundrel who was a pimp called me and asked for help. Four Albanians ambled into his nightclub to mug cash from him, he was afraid to call the police because his establishment was illegal. It was about half past three in the morning.

I arrived at his place, the owner of the saloon said that they regularly rob such places. I had only knucks, and 'I was thin and coughed'. I was 2 meters tall, weighed about 80 kilograms and looked funny. But, any weak predator is stronger than a healthy chicken.

 I entered the club; there was a hulk of about 130 kilograms weight, pumped up and healthy like a bull, and three muscled dudes crowded behind him. I had no chance at all. Freedom means the right to respond to injustice, everything else is slavery.

So, I squeezed the knuckles behind my back and did not know what to do with him, and how to fight against four at the same time. I was not a professional boxer or karate-man. I approached their leader, this main bull, and politely asked him to go outside. He turned his head to me and told me to go into the asshole, in our language it sounded like fuck yourself.

And that's what happened in one moment: my temples exploded and my head burned! It was a feeling as if I were on fire. He turned around to knock me out, but I ducked under his right hook and with all my strength, stroke his temple with the knuckles. He collapsed on the floor, I rushed at him, began to smash him with all my strength on the head, like a pig, I swam in blood, his body twitched in convulsions, I turned him over on his stomach, and pulled his head back with both hands. The barmaid jumped on me from behind and begged me not to kill him in the house.

I was all covered with blood, I felt that my eyes were black, my hands were not shaking. I realized that I was a predator. His friends were standing dumb, paralyzed by this spectacle. I looked calmly at the petrified Albanians, and sent everyone a clear signal: I am a dangerous predator, and you should not crap on my face, send me to fuck or offend my family.

I approached his friends, they were frozen with fear, and quietly told them to go out; and they obediently went out. Why did they go out? What has changed? I took the bull by the legs; he was unconscious and covered in blood, and I dragged him to the exit. That was not easy. I opened the door and threw him downstairs, his body rolling and tumbling down over the steps.

I went back to the club, and the world changed; they took my jacket, and began to wash the blood off, then offered me a drink. Fear has captured all. The barmaid said the question had not yet been resolved, because his brothers would arrive. I was waiting. At least 20 minutes passed and some sturdy guys appeared on the camera monitor, they were ascending to us. The door was armored and the barmaid did not want to open. I told her not to be afraid. I opened the door; I had brass knuckles behind my back.

A bully adult man looked at me very seriously, I answered him more than politely, sorry, we are closed, come back tomorrow. They turned around and left. I went to the bar and happily said to the barmaid that they had gone away quietly and without a fight. She told me to look in the mirror. I went to the bathroom where there was a good light, and I saw only my eyes, my whole face was smeared with blood, my hair was soaked with blood and stood on end.

I understood why the men left. Attitudes towards me have changed. Everyone saw the blood; the chickens have sniffed the predator. This pimp, his name was Kurt Denner, did not even know what to say. He just silently went home. Personally, I did not understand his reaction. The issue with his debts was growing. He did not want to pay and gave me his *Mercedes* as a pledge. *Mercedes's* number was *three sixes.* I made a remark to him that it was unseemly driving around with such numbers on the license plates because God can punish for this...

Then I heard an answer on a million dollars, which he himself remembered, he said that there IS NO God and that he himself was a god. It was his grave mistake, and he repented it later. God very much IS, but it was too late. The first word is worth ten next. Such words must not be even thought in your head, and God forbid to say aloud that the Creator does not exist.

This is a very grave sin.

Unforgivable sin.

God severely punishes for this blasphemy within the lifetime of the sinner and after his death. For what else does God punish? God punishes us for inaction. Yes, a man who truly, with all his heart and soul, believes in the Lord God and is not afraid of anyone except God, this man should not fear other people or death, or Lucifer, for God controls everything and only God decides our destinies. God sends a very difficult life to a sneaky and unbelieving person because he is like a traveler without a compass in the deep jungle. My friends, the main thing is to want to get close to God and God will help you find your way, the path without fear and doubt. This will be a beautiful life, for God knows better than we do our needs, and what is better for us in order not to get lost.

Indeed, *Allah is great*! *Allah* means God in Arabic, as in German it is *Gott*. The Germans believe in *Gott*, that is probably why they are called Goths. God has many names; the main thing is what we mean by saying **God**. God is not a man of blood and flesh, God is the energy that controls everything, the matter and time and all other things.

 After all, no one gives much thought to the fact that our planet moves constantly in a single orbit around the Sun for billions of years, without changing its trajectory. The linear speed of our planet is 108,000 kilometers per hour! Money is just paper, our life is a trifle fraction of time, all that seems nonsense! Try driving a car at a speed of 50 mph to drive exactly on the same track at a miserable distance of, say, 10 miles, two times in a row. You will see. ***This is God!***

My friends, open your eyes wide and go back to God, be honest and do not fool yourselves because nothing happens by itself. An object possibly must not move along a single trajectory for billions of years at a speed of 30 km per second. Our Star the Sun is one of the smallest stars in our galaxy. For those who doubt, there is scientific evidence.

The diameter of the Galaxy is about 30 thousand parsecs or about 100,000 light years, or 1 quintillion kilometers, with an estimated average thickness of about 1000 light years. The galaxy contains, according to modern estimates, from 200 billion to 400 billion stars.

So let us see first what a light year is.

The Light year is a distance that light travels for a year, which is about 10 trillion kilometers or 63,000 astronomical units.

The Astronomical unit is the distance between the Earth and the Sun; that is nearly 150 million kilometers.

Light travels this distance in 8 minutes.

There you are my friends, I think you understand that Someone has created all this, and not just created, but made Galaxy alive, keeping together, and moving at a crazy speed. There are over 400 billion stars such as our Sun in it. Now really, you, Man, will you not kneel before the Creator of such a great beauty? Moreover, there are hundreds of billions other galaxies. My friends, come to believe in God, acknowledge Him and His Greatness, kneel and pray.

Otherwise, God will reincarnate you for thousands of years in a row and you will not escape from the Earth, you will live on the Earth forever in the dark. If you accept my message seriously, then on the Earth everyone will live decently, dutifully serving his sentence. Our souls are shackled in our bodies, we are imprisoned. Nevertheless, Lucifer embellishes our world, so that we are attached to the material values, and do not strive for the spiritual life by the Will of God.

When do we appeal to God? Only when we are breathing our last? This is not right. We should always honor the Lord God and pray to Him because all which happens to us is in order to make us truly believe in Him and never go astray. God confuses people in order to select and take to Himself the strong, and the weak souls will remain on the Earth until they grow stronger and are able to return to God. Earth is both a prison and a school for us. So a man can become free only with God, and this is not my thoughts only, this is a fact. How did I come to God? It was a long and not easy path, my parents were atheists and therefore there was no one to teach me.

Let us go back to 1999, to Germany, the city of Freiburg. 'My comrade' Kurt Denner schemed villainy against me and sent two dudes to maim me. But I always carried a knife on me.

One day I and an acquaintance of mine Anton have just arrived at the house where I lived.

Anton and I had just got out of the car when suddenly some moron rushed at me near the entrance door. I bounced and pulled a knife out of my pocket. He stopped, another dude came up, and they tried to attack me from both sides. While they were pondering what to do next, my friend Anton managed to pull a bat out of the trunk and smashed the first putz on the head. The second jerk ran away. I went up to this motherfucker as he lay on the ground, while conscious, shoved the knife under his chin and demanded why he attacked me. He replied that Kurt Denner paid them to beat me up. All became clear to me. I let the loser go free. My thoughts overcame me. I was thinking about how to solve the problem with this bastard. At that time, Kurt belonged to the *Hell's Angels* gang, and I realized that there were too many of them and one knife was not enough to put an end to this mayhem.

Time passed, I lay low for a while, limited communication with everyone, found other people and worked. I had a daughter. I understood that my freedom was over and I had to live in peace to raise children. I did not put much hope on my wife, because I was looking after the child, I cooked, cleaned, and got up to my daughter at night. My ex not only never helped me, but also shifted all her mother's responsibility to me. After some time I went to a restaurant where different people gathered, occasionally Kurt Denner would drop into this restaurant. I frequented this place to have a small talk with the chef, I can say, we were on warm friendly terms. The chef was French, served more than 10 years in the French *Légion étrangère*, retired and did what he loved and could do best. He was an excellent cook. I accidentally met him downtown, and he told me an interesting story. Lately, he had at the restaurant Kurt with his gang, and they talked about me. Kurt said that he would not leave me alone, and he had two options for me; the first was to frame me up and pack into jail for a long time, the second was to kill, and send my wife and daughter to a brothel, where they would be in brisk demand. I listened carefully to my friend chef and realized that the bastards did not want to live in peace.

Above all is the Will of the Supreme! For not a single hair falls from your head if God does not want it. I called Kurt and asked him to pick up his **three sixes** Mercedes and that I could not afford this car. He had swallowed the bait and immediately arrived. I gave the car away and told him that I had no money at all, I was deep in trouble, and had no cash even to buy diapers for my newborn daughter.

<u>Never be afraid of your enemy, no matter how strong he may seem to you!</u>

Then at this meeting, Kurt told me that he had a kind of a job for me, so I could have good loot, and thus he would return me a part of his debt. We went to a restaurant; he told me that it was necessary to muscle in on some notary, for that Kurt would pay me 20 thousand marks, which equals nowadays about the same sum in euros. Kurt immediately ran to fetch me from the bank 10 G marks as an advance. I agreed. He promised to bring the weapon the next day. I was waiting for a call. I took the car that no one knew and arrived at the meeting place an hour before the meeting itself.

<u>Always be on alert! Pay attention to the tiny trifles and analyze what you see, calculate the situation!</u>

I drove to the parking lot near the railway station and watched people and the situation in general. I knew that Kurt was preparing a setup. In the parking lot half an hour before the meeting, I saw an elderly woman sitting on a bench at the parking lot. In general, in Germany, you cannot see anything like this, like that *Oma* sitting in the parking lot at the *Bahnhoff*. It began to rain, really heavy, but the grandma was still sitting in the rain. It came to me right away, that fag was going to set me up.

Years later, I learned that he was a permanent police rat. But then I did not know this, but seeing that old lady in the rain, I put it all together at once. An inconspicuous grandma in the rain.

Kurt arrived and pulled out a bag, there were two .38 *Berettas* and a sawn-off shotgun. I warned him that we had been being watched, but he just grinned and said that if I did not want to do the job, I should return the prepay. Though this was my money, I did not argue with him, because he owed me a lot more than ten thousands. I put the bag with the weapon in the car. The parking lot was immediately merging into the underground public garage, and I dived in there and right away drove out from the other side of the station. I was heading to the university's underground garage, where I had long ago loaned a parking space and a car. I had a secret store place in this car. Officially, I did not sign down any rent papers; the students were far from being paranoiacs, so everything was arranged without any redundant questions. Without any suspicion, I paid a student from Brazil for six months in advance and kept in the trunk of the car everything prohibited by law. I pulled out the bag and quickly threw it into my *Volkswagen*, which stood parked for more than half a year on this parking lot. Then I easily drove out from the other exit. After leaving the Uni parking lot, I headed to France, to Colmar. On my way, I did not notice the tail, but at the exit from the *autobahn,* I noticed a strange thing. I saw a *Smart* standing in the middle of the road before the turn and it seemed to me very strange, because in Germany people always know where they are going, either to the right or left, no other options. This *Smart* followed me at some distance. I already understood everything and was ready for everything, and I had nothing forbidden in the car. Before the border, there was a small ring turnaround, and I drove up and saw that a *Mercedes* with the emergency stop lights on. I stopped; a flower delivery van pressed against my car rear bumper. All were honking, and I was standing. Then the *Mercedes* began to move little by little, and I saw where I could drive through. As soon as I drove up past the *Mercedes*, a man jumped out of it and aimed a gun at me. I wanted to drive this bum through, but the Special Forces commandos surrounded me from all sides, all in masks and with machine guns, and all at the full parade. Everybody shouted at the top of their lungs. This was how *SEK –Sondereinsatzkommando,* the German special police forces worked. I was ordered to put both hands on the ground. I put my hands on the asphalt; they dragged me out of the car, put plastic loops tight around my wrists and rolled my jacket over my head. Then one of the police officers came up and stepped on my head. I laughed. I laughed because I had foreseen it all.

Almost each of us has a sixth sense, an intuition, but we rarely listen to it.

The second policeman came up with a camera and took a shot of my face. I had enough time to tell him that if he needed my photo, then he could ask me for it without all this circus. I was laughing openly. After about ten minutes, I was lifted up and with a jacket rolled over my head dragged to the police car. I was brought to the precinct, stripped down and shut naked in the infirmary. I banged on the door with all my force and cursed until the door opened; I demanded a blanket, wrapped it around myself and went to sleep on the concrete floor. I was awakened by the officer who the day before got out of the *Mercedes* and aimed a gun at me. He introduced himself, showed his ID, he turned out to be the special police commissioner with all the powers. This department was similar to the FSB or the US FBI; this hencoop was called *BKA – Bundescriminallamt.* Those guys knew their job. They were capable of anything.

Therefore, the first question he asked me was the bag question. I smiled and asked if all this jazz was really because I probably exceeded the speed limit on the autobahn, and said that my bag was there, in the trunk.

The commissar was a cheerful man, he told me, he needed a bag with weapons that I was given at the station.

I answered, "Really, at the station, somebody gave me a bag, but I passed it to the *Oma*, sitting in the rain".

We laughed together. He understood me, and I understood everything too. They searched my apartment through and found a pistol shaped as a ballpoint pen and my glorious knucks. The policemen were not grudging and fined me 3,000 marks or 3 months in prison. I paid the fine.

They tracked me in a helicopter! That was why I did not see the tail. I returned home, where my scared to death wife was waiting for me. She was dragged to the precinct in a bathrobe and interrogated too. Luckily, she did not know anything, because she had been sleeping or eating all the time during our marriage, and was not interested in my affairs at all.

After all, after I had recovered from the shock, I called Kurt. I demanded that we should meet. He had pissed his pants, I could tell it by his voice. Ah, Kurt, it makes me so sorry that the maggots are already devouring you!

I met this pimp and again urgently demanded my money back; demand was my word. He did not ask me anything, neither about the bag nor about the arrest. He gave me the money for a fine. At least that was something. I went to the restaurant where pimps and the whole gang of *Hell's Angels* gathered. I ordered a meal and specially called for my friend, the French chef.

I hoped that maybe he had any information for me. The Frenchman told me, "I am a soldier, I have killed many, there are weapons, and if you want, I will go with you, and we will kill them all."

I was afraid and doubted. Where should I hide my wife and daughter? This was a real burden for such maneuvers. Remember, my friends,

If you want to smash someone's head, do not restrain yourself, go against all, otherwise, anger will devour you from the inside! Fight your enemies, if you want to be healthy and have healthy decent children! And do not fear anyone, except God!

Sometimes we need a clue, and I saw such prompt in an ad promoting some product; they demonstrated a billboard with the slogan: "Good luck goes along with courageous people!" I realized that this is as a message to me personally'; I went to the airline ticket office and bought a ticket to Athens for my wife and daughter. When I came home, I explained that I had faced some problems, and we should leave. My wife's mother lived in Greece, so I sent her with our daughter to her mother. In the meantime, I spread the rumor that I was leaving because I had no money, and no work either. I knew that this information would reach Kurt. I spoke with particular hope that Kurt's best friend, the former police supervisor over illegal drug traffic, some Fridolin Stoss, would pass the word over to him.

Fridolin was a hardcore cocaine addict, due to which he was dismissed from the police with disgrace. Fridolin Stoss was a clinger; he extorted money from pimps and drug dealers, consumed cocaine himself and used prostitutes. He was one of Kurt's close friends, and he always informed Kurt whenever possible.

For all my acquaintances, I left Germany. I have transported my house belongings to Anton's, a student from Moscow. I was preparing for the war. A friend of mine Zhenia lived and studied in Munich. I went to school with Zhenia, later we studied in the same group at the university. Zhenia arrived by a car with the Munich registration. It was a new *Ford Mondeo*. I drove this car and kept Kurt under the close observation. My soul demanded a vendetta for everything. So, with God's Will, everything fell into place, I had a .38 *Heckler Koch* and a wig. I knew what I would do with Kurt. I went to the hardware store and bought a builder plastic hammer. A *plastic* hammer so that this scum would not kick the bucket at once, because it would not be fair. Many times, I imagined in my mind how I smash him on the head. I strike him, and he would not die, and would not lose consciousness, he should enjoy all the pain. He would feel how his bones break, and it would slowly reach his mind that he is not a shiny god, but an ordinary wicked pimp and a dirty scumbag of a moron. He would understand that that was his end, he would at last pray for God's help, ask for repentance, but God would be in no hurry to help. I drove up to the dairy, there were cameras everywhere, so I put a heap of things on me to appear grosser and put on a wig. He always left his house in this street.

Oh, yeah, I forgot to tell you where I got a fashion wig...

A year before these bizarre events I met a girl, Ira by name; she was from Donetsk. Her mom was sick, and she worked in some German family as a housekeeper to help her mother with money. The family moved to Canada, and she was left without work. She asked me to find her a job, and I turned to Fridolin Stoss, presuming that he, as a police officer, could find another family for her. He fixed her a job of an administrator at the disco. Time passed, and I met Ira in an elite club, she was very well clad, sat alone and drank a cocktail. I sat down and said hello. It seemed to me that she hardly recognized me. I wondered how she was doing. She did not tell me everything at once; she was a tranquilizer addict. It happened like that. She worked as the administrator, then she was invited to a corporate party, there was *'my comrade'* Kurt Denner, they drugged her drink and had her gang-raped. Since that time, she worked in a brothel and used tranquilizers daily. I got very upset. So, when I put on my disguise, I remembered Ira, called her and asked if she had a wig. She met me and brought me a wig. That was how I got a wig.

I waited in the car near his house wearing a wig. I waited for hours. Nothing happened; there were no cars. Desperately I turned around to leave when I saw Katya, Kurt's roommate, and concubine.

In Germany, it is not advisable to stand in one place for a long time; the police can drive up and offer their help, which I did not need. Katya killed the engine, and I jumped out and got into her car. She was scared. I was in a wig and with a gun. She knew who I was. Knowing their family life, I played on it. Katya was a prostitute, and she, just like the others, offered her services around. Accordingly, Kurt treated her like a whore. Nevertheless, Kurt was afraid that his property might be confiscated, and therefore he registered his possessions in Katya's name. I knew all these nuances.

I simply told Katerina that if she helped me, I would not kill her, and all Kurt's property would remain to her. It worked. Katya turned off the anti-break-in alarm and led me to the bedroom where that bastard Kurt Denner was sleeping. He always took sleeping pills before bedtime because he was tormented by insomnia. And there he lied with the back of his head turned to me. What a glorious moment God sent me! Just in case, I pulled out a gun not to make anyone laugh. But he was sleeping. I stroked his head, he turned and opened his eyes.

I asked him, "Do you remember me, my brother Kurt?"

And when I saw in his eyes that he was awake, I lowered the plastic mallet with all my force on his head. It went in with a loud crack down to the very handle. The sound was unmatched, unique. My feelings were incomparable even with the hottest sex. I felt a strong euphoria. When I pulled out the hammer, it came out with blood and particles of his brain, the gray matter stained my virgin hammer. I took my time. I watched. He tried to get up, and I gave him that opportunity. Immediately I thought that it was better for him to lie back down and shot through his knee; he fell. There were handcuffs near the bed, probably for the bed pleasures, I took advantage and handcuffed him.

I saw hatred in his eyes, and thought it was high time to beat the shit out of him. I started jumping on his head with all my strength, then lifted it and kicked with all my strength. I had combat boots on my feet, but I felt pain in my leg. I hit him so hard that he flew over the bed and I hurt my leg. I went around the bed to look at him, but I saw the hope of retribution in his eyes. Hope had to be destroyed too, so I hit it with a hammer in the eye, probably breaking more of the skull bone, he lost his eye. And to my joy, he did not lose consciousness, because he swallowed tranquilizers. He was getting all the buzz from the first person.

The freak was a strong guy who earlier fought in the boxing competitions, he had a fucking lot of health. He even surprised me later. But then I recalled that he visited the dentist and made new dentures for himself, I thought that he would not need them anymore, and began to crush his jaws with my hammer. The hammer cracked. The hammer could not stand it.

Kurt Denner was lying on the floor of his bedroom covered in blood and with his head fractured. I leaned over and started kissing his face and stroking his head, I asked him how did he feel himself, if he was okay. He wanted to say something, but just a mumble came out of his mouth. I looked at him and admired him, the insolent and haughty glance was gone, there was no tough guy who even the police were afraid of. I put my life against his life, it was God's judgment, and I was ready to die at any moment. I really wanted to skin him off, for everything he did to me and other people. He was an utter scum and rascal. He had 750 thousand dollars hidden in the kitchen behind the wall, I did not know about it, and I did not care. I came to him, not for money. His bed mate Katya was sitting on a chair in another room and did not move. It was a shock for her. After I kissed him on the face and asked how he was doing and heard an unintelligible murmur, I struck him two more times on the head with the cracked hammer and left him there to turn up his toes.

I wanted him to think all his affairs over before he would go to push daisies, before God would transfer his soul into the body of a manure fly. Although God might forgive him, no one knows. Allah is great and can forgive anyone, even a hardcore scoundrel. God punishes and forgives and God's decisions remain unknown to us. There is a Hadith about a robber, to whom God forgave everything, because he asked his body to be burned, and dispelled after his death in the world so that God could not collect him together and summon him to the Trial. I have crippled many people, but I also have helped many people just like that, for nothing. When I feel the fire and hammering in the temples, I know that I have the right to act. So, I told Katya that we were leaving for France, I put Katya in the passenger seat, she was in stupor, and absolutely obeyed me. As soon as I left, I saw a police raid right in front of me, I was covered in blood, with a broken hammer smeared with Kurt's hair, brain, and blood in one pocket, a smoky pistol in the other. I understood that it was impossible to turn back, it would obviously attract attention, and they would follow me. I could not escape. Thus, I made a cheerful face and went straight into the hands of the police. I did my job, and then let the sky fall onto the earth. The police ordered to pull over, the speechless Katya sat next to me, smiling dumbly. I said that we were going home from the disco, and I was sober. They looked at me and let go, I drove to France, on the way I stopped and ordered myself an underdone steak with blood. I realized that I was not a herbivore. I felt an extraordinary surge of strength, something that seemed unreal, came true. I wiped my feet on the local tough authority guy whom local people were afraid of and made up legends about.

In Strasbourg, I landed Katya and gave her money for the train. Then I left the car in the parking lot and went to Milan. I could not walk normally; my foot was hurt and aching. Probably I had crack in a foot bone from kicking 'my dear friend' Kurt on his head. In Milan, I found a pharmacy and showed them my foot; they gave me a bandage and an anesthetic ointment. I rode in the first class to Ancona and took the ferry to Patra. The seats on the ferry were too expensive and I got into a regular class where there were chair seats just like those on a bus. My foot ached and I had a terrible headache too. I limped to a restaurant where I met a Russian Greek; he was a long distance trucker and transported his vehicle to Patra.

Life is certainly an unpredictable thing. God gives us as we need. At the exit from the ferry, there was police control; I passed it without any problems. My new acquaintance trucker drove me along all the way almost to Athens, to the settlement where the Pontians mostly lived. The Pontians were Russian Greeks who returned to their historical homeland. Greece is a scrap heap and a bunch of every sort of crooks.

I lived about six months in the center of Athens. This was in Platia Omonia, the place where the scum from all over the world came to. Then I did something very stupid. I had contacted my former classmate, who informed on me to the police. So, on the 12th of December, I was arrested by the police at the exit from my house on a tip from Interpol. Two days before this event, I had a dream that my father was mistaken for me and arrested instead of me. God sent me a sign, and I knew it. I lived in Athens in the 7th floor and always went up and down by elevator, but on the day when I saw this dream, two days before my arrest, I climbed upstairs on foot and saw a German sim card on the steps. I knew they fell on my tail. I came home and told my wife that we must hit the road; otherwise, the cops would arrest me. She raised a scandal that I want to dump her and my daughter, that I am irresponsible, etc... I figured, let it be what it should be. Exactly two days later, I walked out on the porch with a baby carriage, and some guy pointed a gun at me; I was slightly drunk and wrested the gun from his grasp, but I had no time to use it, they jumped at me from all sides and took to striking me and twisting my arms. They shouted something incomprehensible which I did not understand. My cow wife just stood and watched. Then the saleswoman, from whom I usually bought hot buns and always eagerly left her the change, rushed on the police and began to hit them with a stick. I watched, tears flowed down my cheeks, I thought, why God did not give me such a live wife as this bun shop girl. I knew that I would not see them again. They pounded me soundly all the way, but I didn't care, I was very offended because my bitch wife just gazed and didn't even move her finger. I was hurt because I knew that I had to flee, but I stayed. Stay for whose sake? In the precinct, I rushed on the cop who shouted rough stuff to me in English. I rammed him with my head, he collapsed, I managed to kick him in the stomach, yelling *'fuck you!'* Then a whole army of police officers ran into the office, along with the police chief. The police chief kicked me hard in the stomach, and I fell. I was handcuffed. Then they spoke a lot in their own language, and the police chief gave a slap on the cheek to the cop whom I had beaten. I never saw him again. After that, nobody insulted or beat me anymore. Then the chief showed the orientation on me. There it was written in English *'Killed people with the hammer'*. Sort of killed a lot of people with a hammer, in the plural. They did that on purpose so that the lazy Greek cops would move around faster.

There was a new stage in my life, a new round; they drove me to the prison into the building Delta, reserved for the dangerous and prone to escape prisoners. They gave me a tattered piece of foam rubber; it was my mattress. The Corridalos Prison was certainly a hard school of life. My cell was number 86; they kept there Russian-speaking cons. They treated me to moonshine, which they distillated from oranges. I shook hands with everyone; the men were different. The informal supervisor among the Russians was Leonid Fitozov, a normal man, quick-tempered, but fair. After some time, we understood each other and lived peacefully. But our acquaintance began not so pleasantly.

The next day some Serozha nicknamed Moldovan approached me. I sat on my bunk and read. I read to disconnect my brains from this madhouse. Serozha came up closely so that I could not get up, and told me to washed the dishes. I politely replied to him that I would gladly have washed the dishes if I had eaten with them. He told me a couple of rough things, so I punched him in the groin. He crouched, I got up and started kicking him with all my might. Serozha passed out, I dragged him into a corner and removed from view so that he was not visible from the corridor. There was no one in the cell, everyone was on the walk, therefore, no one had seen this incident. I went out into the corridor down to the courtyard, sat down on a concrete block and continued reading. My heart was bounding and gave me no peace, I knew that the consequences were coming. An hour later, some guy came up to me and told me to go upstairs, there Lenya wanted to talk to me. I knew there would be trouble. All this time I was protected by the Lord God. God has always been with me. Leonid gathered all his Bandar-logs, there were about fifteen people and organized sort of a powwow concerning the incident with Serozha Moldovan. Lenya was a quick-tempered man, so he didn't go deep into the matter, he wanted to control every conflict and didn't like it when fights happened without his presence or permission. He asked if this was my work with Serozha, I said that was mine. He didn't think twice and immediately hit me in the face, my head started to simmer and I felt very mad that he didn't even try to understand. I immediately warned him and swore to all the saints that if he raised his hand to me once more, then I would grab him and would *'jump down'* with him. And as in the building Delta there were no nets between the floors, many prisoners *'jumped down'*. There was not a single week, when a fresh corpse would be taken out of our Delta, someone would hang himself, someone would *'jump down'*, or someone would poison himself.

A Greek mobster Theodor, who called himself Russian-like Fyodor, Fedia was poisoned with pasta. He killed 16 policemen during his detention; Fedia was armed with machine guns and treated everyone to cold lead generously. Fedia was a real tough guy. A German thief Jurgen Schwartz has poisoned him. Fedia had a lot of enemies, from another Greek family, which Fedia and his family disturbed very much. Fedia had brothers and the father, they all were killed in a shoot-out at the same time; Fedia overslept and missed the gathering, so they did not manage to kill him. He learned from the TV about the death of his brothers and father. He knew the gangsters who were involved in the killing, so he had armed himself and went for the hunt, but there was already an ambush, the police had been waiting for him. Fedia was with his friend, and together they laid down a lot of people.

A bullet with a displaced center of gravity fatally wounded Fedia, the bullet entered through the kidney, and went out between the fingers and damaged all the organs inside, he lost a lot of blood, lost consciousness, and then they arrested him and put in the Corridalos. Fedia made friends with the Russians only, because he did not believe the Greeks. Jurgen was probably well paid for that. Although it might be that Fedia thus escaped from prison. Because he asked me how to escape from the jail, I gave him many examples and one of such was to use a drug that slows down the heart beating. Doctors would not be able to determine the sickness and he would be taken immediately to intensive care, there one should replace himself, and let be buried. Maybe this was possible, but this drug did not cause vomiting, and Fedia vomited. So the truth we would never know, I only knew that Jurgen circled this date in red pencil in his calendar. Moreover, when, a few days before this incident, I asked Jurgen who had a holiday, he was frightened and hid the calendar. Then everything became clear to me. At that time, the famous Vladimir Tatarenko served his term with us, he lived, albeit in a different building, but I often met him in the library, he was a librarian at that time and wrote poems. He gave me his book with an inscription.

There were fights if not every day, then every other day. There were a lot of Albanians and Romanians, they packed together in gangs and constantly clashed. I would not advise anyone to end up in hell of the Corridalos Prison. This, of course, was a bunch of insane, foolhardy and evil people.

So, I was on my own, they wrote about my detention in Greek newspapers in a fantasy style, as of a dangerous psychopath, the raving maniac arrested and defused. A guy named Aleko, one of the Russian Greeks, who served for the double murder, approached me, and told me to keep away from normal people, because they do not communicate with *'chikatilo'* psychopaths. Chikatilo was a notorious Russian serial slaughterer nicknamed *'The Rostov Ripper'*, who in the '80s had murdered more than 60 people and was executed. I did not insist. I had books, and I read. In a month, I read everything in the library. I had to turn to Jürgen Schwartz, he had German magazines, and I read everything along. I smoked a lot, and decided to quit smoking, once I was sick for two days in a row and dumped smoking at that time. This is how the prison benefited me. The prison made me very strong. I signed up for church and began to train; I pumped off the floor. Our chaplain was a real Man of God, he also lived in prison and he had keys from everything; he was old, under 80 years, he had a very long beard and he was carefully bypassed and respected by all the cons. He was kind of an untouchable, when he spoke, everyone obeyed, and he was an unusually strong man. He had a big wooden cross and a very powerful energy; he drove the prison guards out of the church with the words, *'get out, you, children of Satan!'* Everyone laughed and loved him like a father.

The warden, who had himself been in prison for two years, then became the prison governor and walked in shorts around the prison. His body was all in tattoos. This is almost unbelievable and this would have become possible nowhere. But not in Greece. He walked with security, four burly hulks, in formal suits and with guns, and he strolled along in shorts. He felt at home. Years later, they would decide to arrest him, and he would barricade himself in prison. Greece is certainly an amazing country. An American criminal would run away from prison, he dressed himself as a lawyer and left together with his lawyer. Gone clear.

Then I served with the guy Costa Pasaris, this guy was certainly a psychopath, he killed many people, he ran off on the way to court and was caught in Romania, where they gave him a life sentence. This all happened in 2002. One day I walked into the shower and saw a man who had hanged himself and was dangling there naked and all blue. The sight of course was very impressive. Many people have died. There were no windows in the prison; all windows were dismantled. The cons made tables and body armor of plastic glass. They also made knives and daggers of any metal available. Everything was disassembled, so if it rained or snowed, and there was snow in December, everything flew into the cells. We curtained window openings with rags and blankets. Body armor made of plastic very often saved lives. A knife or a dagger slid off the plastic.

I did not mix myself into fights and quarrels. I played chess with the Albanian boss, talked to the German guy Jurgen, who told me about his life. I did not take part in squabbles. Actually, I was on my own waiting for the court. I developed myself a sports program and ran in the yard, pumped off the ground on my fingers and pulled myself up. The grub was unbearable; it was slop. Fortunately, they gave us oranges. Then Lesha began to train with me, a guy who lived with his parents in Athens and wound up behind bars for robbery. He was a calm boy and not conflicted; we ran and practiced every day together. Then Fedia, the one who was later poisoned, joined us. Fedia used to be a professional boxer in Chicago, and then returned to his homeland with his father and brothers, Fedia spoke with everyone in English. Then he began to show us different kinds of the boxers' blows. Unfortunately, he could not move much, his wounds would open, and his nose was often bleeding.

Then one day, I made myself a cold coffee glyco and went out to the balcony. There I saw another bloody mass brawl. I decided to watch this movie. But in this crowd on the second floor I saw Lesha, he was pressed to the railing and was smashed on his head with a piece of iron pipe, he was all smeared in blood. I knew I had to save him because we did workout together and were sort of buddies. I dashed downstairs to the second floor screaming at the top of my lungs, the Albanians did not understand who was screaming behind their back and were confused. I broke into the crowd and covered Lesha with my body; there I saw the legendary Leonid Fitozov all smeared in blood too. I grabbed both of them under my arms, dragged them into the nearest cell and closed the door behind me.

The cells opened in the morning and closed for lunch at lunchtime, only an employee of the establishment could open the cell. They were all in blood and decently broken. Leonid started yelling at me, why did I get into a fight. I was surprised, but I promised to summon back Albanians after opening the chamber in the same line-up to continue. Actually, I got in to save Lesha, and took Leonid along on the way. The Albanians just squeezed them and hit on the heads. When the staff came and opened the cell, they took these daredevils to the medical center for stitching, the torn skin with meat hung in tatters, and the prison Esculapians indeed had to darn them just like socks. Strong guys. Any European would have ended in the morgue after such battles.

The guys were sewn up and brought back. I went out with Lesha to the yard and asked him why the fuck he had got into a fight. And he told me that he saw Albanians beating Leonid, there were too many of them, so he decided not to leave him alone. Thus, you can immediately see who you are dealing with. Most men are just a name, and only very few are decent people. Lesha and Leonid were real and courageous men.

Leonid again summoned all his stooges and called me. I came; Denis began to bother me with stupid questions. I did not answer. I went to Leonid's cell and said, I had nothing to tell him, I was on my own, and had nothing to do with his friendly mob. However, all his pack glare daggers at me; they were jumping out of their socks to get things straight with me. I said in plain words, that their king Leonid was smashed on the head, and all of them stinky cowardly rats meanwhile hid in shit dumpers. It was true. They were ordinary sneaky shit-hearted cocksuckers and had no balls to stand up for their leader.

Denis did time for raping and then killing a girl with an accomplice. This, of course, was no brave deed. Such a sucker like Denis could not discuss me. So when this Denis started talking to me in the wrong tone, I answered him simply. I asked him where he had been during the fight, he hesitated, and Leonid with all his strength punched him in the teeth, and he flew away. I went out.

First, they had to figure it out among themselves. During the walk, Leonid approached me and apologized for having hit me at the very beginning of our acquaintance. I forgave him. He just has stupefied among those moral freaks. I advised him to understand the reason for the fight. It all began because of this Serozha Moldovan. He was an outcast scumbag, his mother tore herself apart between daily jobs to send him money, and he bought vodka from the Romanians and borrowed it too. He paid the Romanians to fetch him grub, two boxes of cigarettes a week, for which his mother paid too. He was an absolutely worthless son of a bitch. That time he began to beat a Romanian, whom he owed money for vodka. The Romanian, though small and thin, heavily punched at Moldovan's jaw with his fist. This idiot Denis saw this and started yelling at the whole prison that Serozha was killed, Leonid ran out and indiscriminately began to thrash the Albanians, who were incidentally standing near Serozha. He thought it was an Albanian who had knocked Serozha down.

Albanians had nothing to do with this. And so the fight began. So I promised Leonid to get it straight with Serozha so that he would not create any more conflicts. Leonid said he would be only glad if I joined their gang, and gave me a go-ahead for any check out with Serozha. This moron was disgusting to me, what with the fact that he wanted to become a thief in authority, with his mother working around the clock, so that Serozha could booze and smoke, and Romanians fetching grub for his mom's money. So I chose the proper moment, took a nylon shoelace from the German and made a loop. I waited for Moldovan to go to the shower. When Serozha had soaped his head with shampoo, I craned over the wall and threw a noose around his neck, jumped off the wall and tied the other end high to the tap. Serozha hung. I went to his shower box, he dangled, kicked, but managed to insert fingers into the loop, so he could still hardly breathe. I hit him hard in the pit of the stomach. I jabbed him so that he swirled on the rope, and I saw that he could lose consciousness. I told him to blink his eyes if he wanted to live. He blinked. I instructed him, that he was just a dung fly, he would pay all the money to the common fund, clean up after himself, fetch grub for himself, redeem all his debts, otherwise I would skin him down. And I would not let loose the rope next time. He blinked his eyes again.

I changed this scum Serozha. He quit drinking and smoking, began to fetch food himself and cleaned in the cell after himself. I made a man of him. Since that time, Leonid gave me the nickname Boa Constrictor. Boa, because my rope was always with me in my pocket. I decided to take up to the collection of card debts at the prison. The Albanian, with whom I have always played chess, agreed to help me. Fedia was poisoned, and I moved from my cell to his place. We constantly trained with Lesha, we still had a TV set from Fedia, and we turned on the music channel and worked out. All calmed down, and everything fell into its place.

Once I returned from the library and saw an old man sitting and sobbing. I approached him and asked how I could help him. I immediately remembered my grandfather Mykola, whom I loved very much. This man knew a little English and said that he was okey, but his brother was put in prison for a long term. His brother was sentenced to 90 years in prison for drug trafficking.

It turned out that this grandpa was a Gypsy Baron. He was very influential, and even in jail, he had a normal civil bed and a Gypsy servant who did everything for him. This grandpa had a mobile phone. Thus, I talked with Grandpa occasionally and unobtrusively, I myself do not like ass shiners, so sometimes I avoided Baron so that he did not think that I was obtruding my friendship upon him. But then an incident occurred, I called my wife on a regular phone, and she burst in tears and said that our daughter poured steaming water on herself. My wife did not know what to do. I went to Leonid; he started calling his friends. My fellow Grandpa saw the turmoil and that I was very upset. I told him about my daughter. He calmed me down and invited me to his place, closed the cell and called his friends, they took my wife and transported her and our daughter to a good clinic and my friend Grandpa paid all the expenses.

I realized that I owed him. The old man said not to bother and did not demand money; he said that it was time for him to do good things. This good man helped me very much with my daughter, he found qualified doctors, and the problem was quickly resolved. Time passed, my birthday came, and I waited for my wife to bring my daughter for a visit. But no one came to see me. I got very upset. Grandpa again saw by chance my sorrow and inquired. I told him that I was waiting for a meeting with my daughter, but my wife did not come. Baron listened to me and advised me to call her. I called and my wife told me that she could not come because she was very busy. I sensed dishonesty. Grandpa said that his wife was lying to me. So he asked me my wife's phone number so that he would find her just in no time. I thought that grandpa just tried to soothe me. But I did not argue.

An hour later, Baron told me that she flew to Germany with some man, and was living in a hotel in the same room with him. At that moment, they were sitting in a restaurant by the lake of Chiemsee. I called again, my wife picked up the phone, I told her not to kill the call, that she was with an Alexander Telman in a restaurant on the bank of the Chimsee lake and living in the same room with him. She hung up and did not pick up anymore. Grandpa turned out to be tough. He told me that in every city in Europe there was a person who does what he tells him. Baron asked me if I wanted him to make a call and they would both be slaughtered at the hotel. I thought it over and over, and then, I said that I did not want my daughter to grow an orphan. Well, he said, then forget it and live on. The old man was very powerful and intelligent. After this incident, I came to him every day and played chess with him. It was very difficult for me to win a party from my friend Baron.

God controls everything and helps us. When everything calmed down, they put me on a plane and sent me to Germany for a trial. My story went on. In Germany, the police were well educated and did not allow themselves to insult the suspects. It turned out that this scum Kurt Denner survived after all, he had a 17-hour operation, and was in a coma. A year later, he came out of the coma and personally attended the trial. Medicine in Germany is very good, their Hippocrates' disciples will soon scuttle through the cemeteries and resurrect corpses. The surgeon said that it was the most difficult operation in his life. My lawyer was a real prostitute who did not know who he was working for. Then one day, I tell him, "You know, I had a bad dream that you were lying in a garbage can with a shot through your head. It is probably a very dangerous job to protect me, I fear for you. I think you should give up protecting me, otherwise, I will feel sorry for you. Sorry to lose you."

A lawyer, Jansen by name, was a complete asshole. I fired him and hired another asshole. They could not do anything useful, most of the lawyers are suckers, they are corrupt and actually do more harm than good. I went on in for sports and reading books. I could have escaped, but I needed money and support outside the prison walls. I did not know anyone who could hide me, so I threw off this option. Then, they put a funny guy into my cell, his nickname was Sunnyboy. He was imprisoned for fraud and theft; he made women fall in love with him and then cleaned their bank accounts. The guy was covered in scars, he looked like he had come back from the war. It turned out that one of his admirers cut him with a knife, he jumped from the second floor onto the broken glass, and after the unsuccessful fall, he was arrested by the police. Sunnyboy told me that I do not need any support being at large, and if I'm lucky, I can arrange everything for myself. In addition, he told me how he escaped from prison in Frankfurt and lived for two years without being caught. I decided to flee because I knew that a very long sentence was in store for me, and they would not add a term for escaping from prison if you did not kill anyone along the way. So I was up to gallivanting off at large.

The simple plan was such, I should get poisoned, and urgently driven to the hospital. Before that, we observed that two guards of the establishment accompanied cons as the escort. I knew that I could handle them. And so I made an incision under my armpit and poured blood into a glass, then stirred it with chlorine bleach for cleaning the floor and drank it to the bottom. It was on Saturday, and I knew that there would be no doctors, and for one hundred percent the guards would take me to the clinic. I called the guard, and when he came, I already started to vomit blood with foam at him. He believed that I felt bad and ran for the orderly. The orderly went into the cell and began to take my blood pressure; it was out of order, my pulse rate, too.

I was poisoned indeed. I was writhing on the floor, the bloody foam was convulsively spitting out of my mouth; I was contorting in agony. It worked. May God forgive me this fraud. They called an ambulance. The ambulance doctors arrived and said that I urgently had to be hospitalized. There was some hitch about who would convoy me out to the *butcher shop*. Lucky me, I heard everything. The patrol police arrived. They looked at me and decided to call for reinforcements. I was swaddled, handcuffed, chained to my ankles, one hand cuffed to the stretcher. Well, that was not exactly what I could imagine about my escape, all bound in chains and convoyed by four armed police officers and two prison guards. I realized that the escape was delayed.

At the hospital, they immediately tried to insert a hose for washing the stomach, but my body resisted and I was fully anesthetized. When I came to myself, it was all over. I was handcuffed to the hospital bed. There was a brigadier beside me. What could I do? So the Brigadier, by the way, he was a normal man, said to me, "If you give me your word that you would not run away from me, then we will walk to the car and go back to the prison together. If you don't give me your word, then I'll call on the radio two police squads, you will be chained and convoyed back to prison. Your choice."

So I made my choice, I gave him my word, and he removed the handcuffs from me and let me get dressed, then put the handcuffs back on and we went through the hospital. And I thought, why the hell I was so stupid. I was bound by my word hand and foot. I could not escape, the brigadier walked ahead of me and did not even turn around. This damned rascal knew that I had no other way. **My word is all.**

I followed him, gazed at the free people around, we walked through the park to the car and I was happy at that moment. God is always with us. God gives us everything from our birth, but we, common mortals do not appreciate this. Now, imagine, if a simple, illiterate peasant is allowed to rule the world, and given a lot of money, then this simpleton would immediately believe that this is exactly the way it should be. See how the new-riches, whom God sent some money, behave. These snobs unavoidably trust in their exclusiveness, they believe that they deserve all by themselves and that they are special, better and higher than others. They are preposterous. But a decent person who knows that God gives everything, this person is not ridiculous. Here, God has given freedom to all, but we do not appreciate it, we understand that only when we lose the freedom. I thought about that when we walked slowly to the car, the brigadier got into the car, and I stood some time near the car and looked at the world, the world that turns round without me. The brigadier was a very decent man; may God bless him, there are few such people.

My mother tells me that I don't remember any good. I remember the deeds, the brigadier did the deed, and I would remember it all my life. Good and evil. Why we people do not remember the good? I will say about myself, it is because there is too little good.

Here I will give an example; a man had helped an elderly woman to cross the road, and after that, he killed 10 people. What would we remember about him? I summarize the number of good and the number of bad deeds, and if the number of bad deeds overcomes, then I do not remember any good deeds. Goodness had faded against the background of all the shit that I received.

My mother raised me. Was that good or it was cowardice? I was bound to become the fifth unsuccessful abortion; they had four successful abortions before. Then what they had to do with me? Kill? I hindered them very much. I was sent away to my dear grandmother and I lived up to 6 years with her. Grandma it was a holy woman! Grandma did not do any bad deeds; she was an angel. Then why my mother says that I do not remember the good? I remember my grandmother very well, remember her good attitude and love her very much. So, may God take my grandmother to Heaven. All the sins, of any gravity, I would be happy to take over for my grandmother, if only God takes her to Paradise. When my grandmother died and lay in the morgue, I kissed my her on her icy forehead and said loudly, let all your sins go to me, I take all your sins, may God prepare You for Paradise.

My mother felt uncomfortable, she made a remark to me. But I replied that this should be earned, that somebody would say such words after one's death. I do not remember the good. I remember my grandmother, she was for me a holy woman, and her word was the law to me. She taught me everything. She always wished me good. The Lord God, I believe, will consider that. But what good did my mother do? I do not remember. I will not take upon myself her sins; let those who remember her good deeds do it. People who love only themselves, will always be alone. My parents will be alone. Grandma called my father and asked if he knew that I was in prison. Father said he knew. Grandma said, go to him, maybe we could help him. If you, my friends, have good parents, worship them and kiss their hands, for God has mercy on you.

At the prison, I was sent to a psychiatrist. The psychiatrist diagnosed a deep form of depression. But as God gives diseases, so God treats us. I was transferred to another prison. At the other prison, everything was relatively normal, without frequent incidents or major conflicts. There I met a Yugoslav pimp there who said that my wife had arrived once and wanted to work in a brothel, but was refused.

A month later, she came to visit me with my daughter. I asked her about her intention to work in a brothel, and she replied that she just went with a friend to look around. Here I will tell you, my good friends, God also gives you a wife. The wife is literally your second half and you need a good half, not a rotten potato. My wife has always been a whore, I just did not want to believe it. Once a guy told me that she had worked at the *Dnister* hotel in Lviv as a prostitute since the age of 17, and I beat this guy. But that was true. She had always been a pussy-monger.

Now she lives in Switzerland in the village of Oberwil with the Italian man named Isidoro. I was very disgusted to hear such a news from a pimp, and I told him that if I hear that again, I would kill him where there was no video surveillance. He was afraid of me, because everyone knew my story. I wonder what she can teach my daughter. She is 16 years old now.

Then they did not allow relative's visits to me anymore. A letter came from the judge that my wife appealed to her and demanded to withdraw my parental rights to my child. The judge asked her directly if she knew where I was, and she replied that she did not know. But the judge knew that she visited me in prison, and decided to let me know about that. She had informed me that my ex came not alone, but with some dude. I told the judge, God was my Witness, that I gave everything to my ex-wife. I dressed her, shod, made her the documents in order to study in Germany. She did not know German, so I taught her German and forged a certificate of knowledge of the language. All I did was for her. She bought brand clothes only; her friends would not recognize her. I sweated out my ass so that she had everything. And there was the result. But the reason was simple. You cannot build a house in the swamp. I was a fool. I would never marry her, but she got pregnant. She assured me for a long time that she had absolute infertility due to prolonged erosion of the uterus. I was a gullible fool. She became pregnant, and I honestly decided to merry her. I was young and stupid, it was not necessary to go to the registrar to become a good father. But, we learn from our mistakes. So in order that we do not learn from our mistakes, parents are obliged to give a good upbringing and education, and then the probability of mistakes is reduced by dozens times.

My ex-spouse, after years wrote a statement to the police on me, she learned somehow that I could be released on terms, and a violation of law was necessary to show in order to cancel my preterm release. 4 years have passed, and the penitentiary authorities already were about to apply the possibility of parole. When they called me to the lawyer, I knew that problems were about to follow. At the lawyer's office, I saw two police officers, those who transported me from Greece. There was a senior man, the chief police commissioner, he was a decent man, and he always treated me with respect, because I did not deny anything, but admitted that I hammered that asshole, and if I could return the time back, I would repeat every stroke again. He liked that I did not wheedle, and said that I hate all kinds of scum and would kill it at the first opportunity.

So this commissioner told me that my ex-wife wrote a statement concerning the alleged threat on my part. I was shocked. I sat silent. The Commissioner said that since they have been strenuously watching me for the last six months, they had not noticed any threats. Oksana said that I called her on the phone and threatened. The commissioner stated that this Oksana's number was already registered and under their surveillance for a long time, and they did not register any threatening calls. They listened this whore's phone round the clock, and came to the conclusion that she wanted to deceive the police. It did not work; the prosecutor annulled the statement and warned her that if she manipulated the law enforcement agencies, she would be brought to justice.

She didn't want me to go out. But, for all is the Will of the Lord God. When I was transferred to a new prison, the prosecutor came to me to talk. And the topic of conversation was that the newly resurrected Kurt, promised reward for my head. The reward was 250 thousand euros. Some Kurt's errand boy carried an advance for the killer, but the killer eliminated the intermediary, grabbed the money and disappeared. He killed Kurt's stooge in Karlsruhe in broad daylight in a street cafe. One pimp with cash less, and Kurt became a little poorer.

The prosecutor warned me to be extremely careful and that there was a hunt cast on me. I thought that it was necessary to change the balance of powers a little. I asked the prosecutor if he knew about the house that Kurt bought himself in France. The prosecutor did not know, but I told him the location of the residence. There was always a lot of unregistered weapons in this house. The prosecutor knew that this information was valuable, so they came to him unexpectedly to his house with a search warrant. They had found grenades, 700 kilograms of explosives, over a million euros of illegal money and a lot of interesting stuff. Kurt Denner was immediately put under investigation, and everything found, naturally, was confiscated.

Kurt has become still poorer. And nobody needed poor Kurt. He was sentenced to a real term, and he very insistently pleaded the prosecutor not to transfer him to the prison where I was serving my time. Kurt was scared to death. Naturally, I would beat shit out of this asshole Kurt every day. The Al Capone game was over. Kurt has become an ordinary convict. I hated him. Kurt was an ordinary suburban rogue who imagined himself a god. He needed a lesson to learn.

What should we do, that God forgives us? We should be clear like children, without envy, and without anger. You have to go through many trials to reach this state. You have to be poor; you have to be rich. You have to cripple and kill many people; you have to forgive and save many people. And when you reach the point where you see that God writes the Book of our lives, then you kneel down before The Lord God. Moreover, you will understand that only God matters and nothing else. It is necessary to go through all the circles of hell so that your soul and your eyes open.

A person who lives a routine life will not come to God. We have to move from point zero to point ten, and if we stand still, we will remain at the station Zero. Sitting in one place, we will not be able to experience life situations that bring us closer to God. Thus, for example, if a person comes to you and asks you to believe him, and says, jump from the roof of a twenty-story building and nothing will happen to you, no one will believe. But if God tells you, "Jump!" then you have to jump, even if you are very scared.

When you believe in God, then there should be no fear. Fear is inherent to an unbeliever. For when a man believes, this man is not afraid of anything except God. When we know God, we must help other souls find a way to God. For, lighting the way to other people, we light our way too. By helping others go the right way, we save ourselves too. Teaching a person to do wrong is easy, but to substantiate for a person why he should live righteously is very difficult. And if a person is an ordinary philistine, then he will not be able to convince anyone. Only an avid hooligan and a sinner will be able to find an approach to any unsophisticated and doubting person. Because any sinner has a lot of life experience and baggage. A philistine does not know anything. A philistine is just empty talk, there is no action and power behind his words. Only a very bad and evil person who despises the law can teach you to love and respect God. Because only a real killer and villain knows who God really is. Other kind people are like chickens, they go to work and lead a spiritually poor life. Their thoughts are only about food and toilet paper. They turn to God only when they are in an ardent need. Only in the face of death, only when the trouble comes, which knocks the chicken out of ordinary life, he appeals to God.

As for the predator who doesn't give a shit about the laws of chickens, he knows that his fate is in the hands of the Lord God every day. The predator knows that only God gives us food and shelter, the chicken thinks that he is presupposed to have food and shelter. That is why most people are chickens because they believe only in the grain that they are given, the chickens see nothing further than their hencoop, the chickens condemn the predators and imprison them as soon as possible or execute them. Chickens do not believe in God, chickens have their own master, and they cannot have two masters. The predator does not have a master who scatters the grain, the predator has his master God. A predator is a free man who fears no one but God.

Believe me, the world will change around you. You will have new friends and your relatives and beloved ones will leave you. Your family may turn away from you. But do not be afraid. Practically, clues are always around us. A proverb says, only dead fish flows with the stream. This is a hint. We need to swim against the stream.

So, the time for the trial came, and Kurt Denner himself appeared in the court on foot, and after all the operations he looked even better than before. He had 17 hours of surgery on his head and a part of the brain was removed, he lay in a coma for over a year. There were, of course, consequences; Kurt got epilepsy attacks. Kurt hired an additional lawyer who supported his accusations against me. In addition to the desire to sentence me for life, the court also fined me 780 thousand euros to cover all expenses for the damage I had inflicted to the complainant. Kurt flourished like after the resort. I grinned in his face. All his friends came to the court. He looked at me and I was smiling. I was glad that I had beaten him and humiliated him. I was glad I was wiping my boots on his face. I morally raped him; I put him down. He could not look in my eyes. He felt sick, and he left the courtroom. I won, and I felt fine, although I understood that the judge was going to throw the book at me. It was too late to play the fool; I showed everyone my true face. My law and my rule are:

**'Even the most venomous snake should be able to play a hose for watering flowerbeds!'**

This is my slogan, I do not threaten the object, I immediately kill without warning, attack from the back, meanly and ignobly. I believe that there are no rules when killing, there is only the result, the one who survives, takes the victim's load. Murder is a burden and a great responsibility, it is possible that all the problems of the deceased are overloaded upon the killer; and it will be necessary to work off. Killing is not just an action, it is a strong motive that prevents us from sleeping, eating and living a normal life. The necessity to kill the target person is like a disease that prevents us from calm living. The prosecutor came to my cell during the break. In each court, there are several cells in the basement for the accused. The prosecutor was a tough guy, a former athlete, and it was clear that he was a decent man. He wanted to know why I used a plastic hammer, why I did not shoot him but hammered him all night long instead of finishing the bastard at once. The prosecutor said that guys from Eastern Europe are always very cruel.

I did not lie to him. I told him the truth that I whacked him, the way you slap cockroaches that crawl on food with a slipper, and I will continue to whack all kinds of scum and carrion. I was created by God to kill scum and carrion. The prosecutor listened to me and left.

Panic attacked me, I thought that I had spoken enough for life imprisonment without parole, and if he recorded the conversation and would demonstrate it to the court, I would never see freedom anymore. Fear fell on me. I realized that I had spoken too much.

It proved to be exactly the opposite. It happened that the prosecutor appreciated my honesty very much, although, he warned me that I was aggravating the situation with my statements. After our conversation, the prosecutor read newspapers and did not enter into the debates at the trial. They tried to activate him with various questions, but he brazenly and defiantly read the newspaper and did not support the dialogues. So, when the judge appealed to the prosecutor about the maximum prison term, the prosecutor replied that he would determinate the sentence of seven years of imprisonment, with the deduction of already served. It was a shock for everyone because earlier the prosecutor demanded at least 13 years and everyone knew that. What has changed? I infected him. I infected him with the John Doe virus. John Doe was a mayhem rogue, who himself decided for whom to live and for whom to die. That was just the way it was, everyone was indignant, so the judge determined 9 years with the possibility of parole. That was the way they decided to punish me.

After arriving at the prison, I embarked on a hunger strike in connection with the measures they took against me. The hunger strike is a very useful exercise that cleanses us both physically and spiritually. I had a very real vision during the hunger strike. When I went on a hunger strike and did not eat for 31 days, then about the 12th day I saw a very real dream. It was as if I were in China or Japan, I lived in a castle, and a servant came up to me and said, "Master, they came for you".

I dressed in violet wooden armor and went out. I had a short sword tucked in my belt and a long sword behind my back. A whole army gathered in front of my castle. All of them were riders dressed in black clothes. There were 312 people; I knew their exact number. They very politely demanded a child from me. I knew they wanted to kill the baby for some reason. I refused them, and they called me out to a battle.

I killed everyone; there was a pile of corpses. I was moving at an extraordinary speed and put all those warriors down along the radius. Of course, it sounds unbelievable. But the dream was very real, in the battle, they pierced me through with arrows, and I also died still standing.

I immediately went to the Court of the Lord, and God said to me, "You killed many people in order to save another's child. I will give you one more chance, but in this life do not kill anyone!" He crushed my soul down to the thickness of the spider web and let current through me. The pain was very strong, indescribable in words. God said, "The pain will be constant if you disobey Me!"

My story sounds absolutely crazy, but there is one coincidence. There are programs on the Internet, where by the date of birth you can learn about your past life. So, I entered my birth date on July 3, 1977, and it turned out that in a past life I was a digger and a warrior who died in an unequal battle. I lived in the south. Thus, if you add up my date of birth, you get 34, which means a warrior who died young, in an unequal battle.

Here is another coincidence. Now, after years, this vision does not leave me no peace. My present wife insisted that I looked for similar stories in history or in legends. After 16 years of the research, I found myself in another life, and everything became clear to me. In a past life, I was Musasibo Benkey, who was a warrior. He defended the honor of his master and killed more than 300 samurais near the castle. He died when he was 34 years old. He was over 2 meters tall and resembled me in appearance. An ancient fresco remained where I was earlier.

At the age of 17, he was over two meters tall; people called him a giant. He was trained in handling naginata. This is a long weapon, similar to a hybrid of an ax and a spear. He left the Buddhist monastery to join the secret sect of mountain monks-ascetics. According to the legend, Bankey went to Gojo Bridge in Kyoto, where he disarmed each fencer passing by and thereby collected 999 swords. During his 1000th battle, he was defeated by Minamoto-no Yoshitsune, and became his vassal, fighting with him against the Taira clan.

Being under siege a few years later, Yoshitsune committed ritual suicide, hara-kiri, while Bankay fought on a bridge in front of the main entrance of the castle to protect his master. The story tells that the soldiers who organized the siege were afraid to step on the bridge to join the battle with the lonely giant. Bankay killed more than 300 warriors, and, long after the battle was over, the samurai saw Bankkey still standing upright, covered with wounds and pierced with arrows. Then the giant fell to the ground, dying while standing, which eventually became famous as "The Standing Death of Bankay."
He died in the battle when he was 34 years old.

You may not believe all this, maybe I was a woman-dishwasher, and maybe I worked in a brothel. But, if this were so, it would undoubtedly have an impact on my present behavior, for nothing passes without a trace. God teaches us the righteous life and the righteous behavior; and we all have been everything: a dog and a cat, and a woman and a Chinese and a Negro, each of us has an unusually large experience; God erased our memories but left habits and skills.
This can be seen in a foster home where children live without parents. We know who the parents of these children are, but the children do not know this and very often, their behavior is different from their parents' behavior. I can judge it by myself; my parents are absolute strangers to me in the mentality, and in faith, and in everything. God has hooked me to them with the purpose of growing a calmer person, but the past still took its toll. I often asked my mother where I came from, what I was

wearing and what things I brought with me. I knew from the childhood that I was a stranger, and they were strangers to me. I always wanted to have a Japanese sword, katana. Where do such thoughts and desires come from? What is their reason? May it be because we had those things in the past life?

God erases our memory so that we do not harm ourselves and not pursue the material aspect in life. If we could remember our past lives, it would change the whole world. No one would **believe** in God, everyone would **know God personally**! And this would not allow a person to sin and will allow a person to realize the Power of the Lord God *alone by himself*. The soul must independently realize everything without compulsion. After all this mundane mud, we must either remain clean or wash off, in order to return to God. So that after all the trials of our enemy Lucifer, we remain strong and on the righteous path.

...Again we are together
Again, He brought me back
Again theft, lies, robberies and murders,
Again life in darkness and heartache
The pain of separation every day…
Again diseases and headache
You make me believe in this hell…
But I know the Truth and I know my home.
You cannot fool me,
I know you, Lucifer, in person.
Protect me O Lord from your faithful Servant!
Forgive me, destroy my soul and do not return,
Do not return me to this hell!
If I deserve punishment, punish and kill,
Just do not bring me back
On this damned Earth.

And I ask you, O Lord, protect me from your prosecutor, the Satan.

It is Lucifer who calls us to answer for what we say. Our tongue is our enemy and it is written in the Qur'an. What you think, remains between God and you, but what you say aloud, Lucifer standing next to you, listens attentively and does exactly as you yourself said. I want to say a few words to clumsy jokers who love to joke about the phrase **Allah Akbar**. *Allah Akbar* in Arabic means **the Lord God is Great**, so what is funny here? Allah, Yahweh, Jehovah, Elohim, Gott, Gat, God, Bug, Bog, Boh – in all languages in different ways.

<u>**Is it possible to laugh at your Creator?**</u>

But one must live to this point in order to understand this. What happens if I kill a common simple man? How will my life change and will it be our will, or will it be the Will of the Lord God? Will He send for the person whom He wants to meet at this moment? How does this happen? Is it by chance? Do we decide our own fate? Are we guided in the right direction? Why decent people are killed, and the blasphemous scum come to the power? Is it really God, Who does it? Why did God need a Stalin? Or a Hitler?

They were needed to try people. What to do when carrion is in power? They were put by Lucifer to create a chain of mortal sins. So that people would steal, rob, and kill one another. When such vampires are in power, it is very difficult for a common person to live according to the Commandments of God. These scums are established by the Devil himself personally, this is his planet, his mundane world, given to him by God, and Lucifer is the owner. Those who survive, he sends back to God, to His Kingdom, and those who are completely rotten, he detains here, on the Earth forever, to be reincarnated every time in a new body. There is no way out, the price is very high. It takes a daring act to break out of this vicious circle. Sometimes, when you look at monks who live in caves and pray, you realize that these souls have comprehended their fate in this world and want to escape.

Tyrants will live here forever. Lucifer sorts them by countries and puts them at chosen times. A man's birth in a poor country in total mayhem is not accidental. This is the result of his previous lives. To be born in a civilized country, among decent people, this must be earned. Those boys and girls who live a carefree life will pay a bitter price. There are no coincidences in life; life is the objective law. Imagine that you live all your life in Paradise, and then you are sent on a business errand to the Earth, you have gone all the way, but you are not allowed to return home, you are tired, but you are sent back. Sometimes I understand why babies cry so much, they swear. They say, "No, O Lord, why?" But God is silent because this is a prison and until you realize everything and comprehend this with your heart and soul, you will be returned repeatedly. How terrible it is. It hurts, it is despair and pain.

You cannot run away from Lucifer, he will find you wherever you hide.

Once, I went to help a farmer Sergey Aksenov, this was in Efremov, Tula region. I had to help collect his debt receipts that fell into hands of local gangsters. While nobody approached him, I started grain harvest with him. I tried to meet with the bandits, but they were not too eager to meet me. We harvested barley and wheat, Sergey was on the combine harvester, and I drove the crop on a *ZIL* truck for sorting.

Prior to that, we tried to catch the swindler who stole gluten and forced a car from Sergey at one time. We failed to catch this scoundrel. We decided just to work in the field. We were all very tired and dirty, but jolly.

Then one day, I asked Sergey's mother to bake us an apple pie and started peeling apples. Unexpectedly two extremely bulky man butted into the house. They were racketeers, Sergey's so called 'roof', and he regularly paid them money 'for the protection'. I was silent. Sergey told me everything. Actually, they did not help him, but took the money regularly. Sergey said that one of those guys, Valera, was present when local bandits demanded from him a receipt and a technical passport for agricultural equipment. I was dissatisfied. I had a .38 *Makarov* with rubber bullets, and I decided to use it. I sat on a bucket and peeled the apples. They spent the night at the neighbor's' and in the morning came back to our house again.

These sleek arrogant mugs imposingly sprawled on the chairs in the kitchen, without taking off their caps. They behaved and spoke impudently, using the criminal argot. Sergey turned gray and almost invisible; he squatted and opened his mouth like a fish. Everything seemed hopeless, and I did not like it; God Almighty knows that.

They did not pay attention to me at all, so I had a big advantage. I pulled out my *Makarov*, prepared in advance, walked over to Valera and asked, "Are you Valera?" Without waiting for an answer, I twice shot him from close range at his head, and next four shots in the chest. In my other hand, I had a big ax; I immediately put it on of another gangster's neck and told him to fish everything out of his pockets with his left hand, and put his right hand on the table. He produced his money, keys, and documents. While he was laying that stuff out, I loaded a new clip into the gun and racked the slide. This second guy just got out of prison on parole and was not ready for such a turn. He asked me not to kill him because he had small kids. They came to themselves and became nearly normal people. I helped them get back into the human form.

Therefore, the most powerful weapon of Lucifer is an optical delusion. We always make mistakes, because we do not always see what we really are. For example, a little boy, an orphan who repented for his sins, has often behind him much more power, than an adult armed gangster does. We think that in front of us is a homeless, stray, crippled dog, but no, this is an angel who has taken the form of this dog. And we stupidly offend the angel, who then by the will of the Lord punishes us. for our ignorance. This is an optical, visual deception. A delusion. Lucifer is the master of delusion.

And here these strong guys who considered themselves tough gangsters wound up in the hospital, that who was most unabashed lost his eye and a liter and a half of blood. Doctors pulled rubber bullets out of the head.

The police arrived, and they told everything except the truth. They told me that I punished them, but they did not say why. The one I shot in the head was still in the hospital, while the second moron already wrote a report to the authorities on me at the police station.

Farmer Sergey was with him there, and warned his father, his father rode me to the field, far from home. It was night and it was cold; I hid the gun in the forest near the field. I froze and I was convulsing with tremor. Cramps went all over my body. I knelt down and prayed. I turned to God; tears flowed down my cheeks. I told God that He had created me like this, and I was not guilty that I am the son of Cain and asked God to destroy me and my soul.

 But it appeared that God loves me, that night God woke up the chief of the criminal investigation department of the Tula region. I did not know that. And this chief for some unknown reason arrived at the police station at half past three. He rejected that written information and instructed this bandit to sign a document that there was self-defense on our part, and he had no complaints in exchange for withdrawing the accusation of racket and extortion. Everyone was shocked, including the police and Sergey. Sergey's father came for me when I had already lost any hope. Sergey's father asked me to find the gun and hand it to the police to close the criminal case. There I was in the forest, in complete darkness, I found the hidden gun. It was salvation from God. The Lord God saved me again. God knows that I do not offend good people; I can only punish a villain.

Therefore, my dear friends, use this life in such a way as to prove to God that we are worthy to be brought home to His Kingdom. Our home is the Kingdom of the Lord God. Those, to whom my words seem funny, let them laugh. But he laughs best who laughs last.

I am a servant of the Lord God. When I read about the Prophet Mohammad, tears came out of my eyes. This man left for us a pattern of righteous behavior. Just like Jesus Christ; but we know little about Jesus because the church rewrote everything in its own way. Catholics and Orthodox want to subjugate people by force and intimidation. The Inquisition destroyed whole peoples, burned innocent in fire at the stake. There is an interesting document; the manuscript known as *The Hammer of the Witches* is a medieval treatise, which describes how pregnant women and young children were burned in fire at the stake. Christianity resembles Satanism, from rituals and priests to homosexuals and pedophiles. These facts are substantially proven. This religion is trying to intimidate ordinary people with the horned devil, while they themselves are the real representatives of Satan.

What do we know about the Prophet Mohammad? This information is available to anyone on the Internet and everyone can read this information.

By the end of his life, he managed to create a mighty state that controlled almost the entire Arabian Peninsula. To rule the state, the Prophet Muhammad appointed governors in different regions. The Prophet Muhammad died in the hejri year 11 A.H., leaving behind the greatest legacy. The Islamic religion, the postulates of which he formulated through divine revelation, had a great influence on the development of world civilization. He led a modest life, was content with only the most necessary things for life. He had many virtuous qualities. He was a fair, meek, forgiving, patient man, distinguished by incomparable generosity and generosity, always kept his promises. Muhammad was also famous for his fearlessness and courage. All these ideal qualities were given to him by Allah, the last Messenger, and Prophet of Whom he was.

Is it really not good for us to strive to live like the Prophet Mohammad?

Christianity is the teaching of Lucifer and I will prove it to you now. Cast away all your prejudices and start thinking logically. First, if we read the Old Testament, we see that all the Messengers of the Lord were great people, and no one had the right to insult those chosen people. King Solomon, Abraham, Noah, Moses, these people were special; they communicated with God and were untouchable. God gave King Solomon two demons to perform the service of his will.

In Christianity, Jesus was crucified on the cross, and all Christians wear the crucifix on their bodies, as a proof that simple filthy little people are stronger than the Messenger of the Lord. And as proof of this, they carry in processions the trophy, the Crucifixion of the Messenger of the Lord God. In other words, they enjoy that He was crucified to redeem their sins and wear the instrument of shameful execution on their chests.

The church rite, The Eucharist is the oblation, eating the body of Christ, and drinking the blood of Christ; what is it, if not a rite of Satanists? The Bible says that

In the beginning was the Word, and the Word was with God, and the Word was God *(John 1:1)*

It is written in the Gospel that Jesus Christ in one word could turn water into wine, and parsons in the church with the same Word turn bread into human flesh and turn wine into blood. Do you drink the blood of Jesus Christ? Do you drink the blood of the Messenger of the Lord? And like carnivorous animals or cannibals devour human flesh of the Messenger of God? Is this not the Devil's mass?

The most delusional thing that I heard is that Christ took our sins upon himself! How shall we understand it? Suppose, I killed a man; would Jesus be responsible for this?

Read what the Prophet of Allah Muhammad said about the Prophet Jesus Christ in the Qur'an. Islam teaches that Jesus is the Great Prophet who is alive and always is with us; the Crucifixion was invented by people. Jesus is the Prophet and the Messenger of the Lord, and not God, as the church instils. He ate and drank, which meant he used the restroom. Therefore, He was a man, a chosen, special man, but not God! God created galaxies, God created time, and the Messengers are our educators and mentors. There is no one but the Lord God. God created everything in the Universe. God cannot be compared with anything or anyone. It is not necessary for God to draw or invent things the way we do because our brain is small and it still works only at 15% of the total power, for some people it does not work at all. God also gives us mind, knowledge, and wisdom. God gives us courage; everything that we have, God gives us.

I read many different books, but no book clearly warns about what awaits us. People are still unaware that they would almost immediately pay for their wrong behavior. No book says clearly and directly that the Supreme Reason records and instantly analyzes all our actions. The Qur'an says that with each person there is a Malik, a personal angel, who notes our actions and conversations. If every person realized this, he would make fewer mistakes, respectively, the way home, to God's Kingdom would be much shorter.

Here, eventually, I will tell you an instructive story. There was a man, who worked in the Prosecutor's Office all his life and always was in power. This scoundrel's nickname was *'Reverend'*. After he was caught on bribery and shamefully fired from the Prosecutor's Office, this pipsqueak went to work as a lawyer. He led an obscene way of life. As a lawyer, he demanded money from poor people but never helped them. People counted on his help in vain, as he was permanently deceiving them. He grew fat and constantly drank a lot of vodka. He lived in comfort and admired very young girls.

One day he met a young single woman, Matilda by name, who had a small daughter, and she hardly could make ends meet. She worked, but her salary was small and Matilda never had enough money. There was no help from anywhere.

In despair, Matilda decided to earn some money and went abroad in search of work. She worked some time at the farm, and did well, so the farm owner decided to help her. He lent her money at one percent to buy an apartment. Matilda was very happy and when she returned to her homeland, she began to look for an apartment. But it was not easy to find a proper living place at once.

 At that time, Reverend worked as a lawyer in a bank. He persuaded Matilda to exchange dollars for rubles and put the money in the bank at interest. Reverend was a very cunning swindler and decided to get a benefit; he knew perfectly well that he was deceiving a lone mom. She exchanged decent reliable money for rubles, the rate of which falls every day and put the whole sum at interest in a bank. God considers what this scoundrel Reverend did. Two months later, the bank went bankrupt. When Matilda turned to the Reverend for help, he advised her to be an appeasable girl, and maybe then, he could help her.

Reverend, who was already under 60 years old, was nevertheless very interested in sex. So this old dirty lewdster told her something like this, "You are nobody for me that I would help you. If you were some local authority, or my friend, or a judge, or a police officer, I would return this money back to you at once, but you are nobody." Of course, this rogue Reverend did not know in his 60 years of age that we are all equal before God. Nevertheless, this is a very important fact that must be considered.

Matilda at that time had been meeting with a local boy, and they wanted to start a family. This young man was very partial to injustice. They knew they were in trouble and worried about themselves. The money was to be returned or worked out. The farm owner arrived from abroad and invoiced. Matilda and her boyfriend were in a bind. She decided to ask Reverend to help her draw up a document to the main office of the bank in order to get back at least part of the money. Matilda was by then pregnant, in about the fifth month. She came to Reverend to his office. Firstly, he took her to the restaurant, expanded before her on all kind of baloney about his life and instructed her about his plans for tomorrow.

Here for the admirers of Bulgakov, I quote him verbatim. This is a dialogue between Woland and Berlioz.

"Now, I dare ask you, what are you doing tonight if it's not a secret?"
"Of course, it's not a secret. Now I'm going to my place in Sadovaya Street, and then at ten o'clock this evening a meeting will be held at MASSOLIT, at which I will be the chairman."
"No, this cannot be in any way," the foreigner firmly objected.
"Why?"
"Because," the foreigner replied, glancing with squinted eyes at the sky, where black birds silently glided in anticipation of the evening cool,"Annushka had already

bought sunflower oil, and not only bought it, but she even has spilled it. Therefore, the meeting will not take place."

That is how profoundly Mikhail Bulgakov understood the essence of things. Mikhail Bulgakov had a direct connection with God and knew the truth.

Reverend expatiated before Matilda upon how he would proceed in his career, what position they promised him, and so on. In the flow of the conversation, he uttered the key phrase that ***God does not matter in his life***. Then, under the pretext of drawing up a document, he proposed Matilda to go to the forest with him, intending to induce her into the intimate communication. Of course, Matilda did not want any relationship with this old fart but she had no choice. Reverend knew that she was absolutely defenseless and knew that he would not be brought to account for it. But in real life, as well as in fiction books, everything happens the same way. As soon as Reverend arrived into the woods, he dragged Matilda to the back seat of his car and tried to tear clothes off her. When Matilda explained to him that she has a young man whom she was going to marry and that she was pregnant, he stroke her on the forehead…

That was it. God forbid to beat a woman, especially pregnant! Then something happened. A man in a black balaclava opened the car and began to deliver heavy blows indiscriminately on the Reverend's head and face with all his strength, and then in the process, he pulled out a pistol and shot him three times between the strikes. Death to the former prosecutor did not come immediately; God did not want this piece of shit to die without serious repentance. He suffered for a long time and eventually went to hell. I think that God will put his soul into the body of a stray dog so that he had enough time to reflect on his behavior and the wrongdoings.

Respect others and consider your words. God sees and hears everything.

I came up with this short story for you, so that you understand that absolutely all people should be respected, regardless of their status and physical form. Be always with God, pray, and God will always help you and protect you from misfortune and from His Servant Lucifer.

Lucifer is the Servant of the Lord, do not blaspheme, and the Prosecutor Lucifer will never come after you.

Epilogue

In this life, God gives us the path that we should stride along. Do not transgress, do not go over the speed limit, do not take shortcuts, you do not need to dice anyone, and you will reach the finish line, otherwise, you will be repeatedly returned to the start. You will be sent back to the kindergarten, to school and you will experience the strive for food again and again. Alternatively, you would be born again as a person of the different sex, or a cripple for life, or appear somewhere in the jungle with a bare ass. There is no need to be cunning; our judge is God, Who sees everyone. Lucifer should not be afraid of, fear the wrath of the Lord God, and fear your stupidity, wrong actions, and blasphemous words. Do good, respect others, control your speech, and pray on your knees with your face turned down towards the floor. And God will give you everything you need, and Comrade Lucifer will make sure that no one could offend you.

God is always with us.